Robert
and the
Troublesome
Tuba

Also by Barbara Seuling

Robert
and the
Troublesome
Tuba

by Barbara Seuling
Illustrated by Paul Brewer

**A
LITTLE APPLE
PAPERBACK**

SCHOLASTIC INC.

New York Toronto London Auckland Sydney
Mexico City New Delhi Hong Kong Buenos Aires

ISBN 0-439-44377-6

12   11   10   9   8   7   6   5   4   5   6   7   8/0

Printed in the U.S.A.   40
First Scholastic printing, March 2003

to Elliot, Andrew, and Robert
—B. S.

for Donna, Ned, and Andy
—P. B.

Contents

Robert
and the
Troublesome
Tuba

The Blank Wrapper

Paul unwrapped a piece of bubble gum and popped it in his mouth. "Hey. Listen to this," he said, reading the inside of the wrapper. "It says my name will be famous one day."

"Yeah," said Robert. "When you change your name to Sidney Famous."

It was an old joke, but they still cracked up over it.

"What about the number?" asked Robert.

There was always a fortune printed on each Bubble-oney wrapper, and sometimes a number. If there was a number, you won that many dollars. All the kids were chewing Bubble-oney bubble gum like crazy trying to get a wrapper with a number on it. Paul looked at his wrapper.

"Nope. No number. Maybe next time," he said.

Robert unwrapped his gum. "Hey! Look at this!" he said. He showed the wrapper to Paul. "There's nothing on it. Not even a for-tune."

Paul looked at the wrapper. "It was probably just a mistake at the factory," he said.

Paul was probably right, but it still felt weird to Robert.

Both boys chewed furiously as they walked the rest of the way to school. They each had to chew three pieces a day to increase their chances of winning. They had one in the morning on the walk to

school, one on the way home at three
o'clock, and the last one at home, after
dinner.

Their book bags were stuffed with Bubble-
oney bubble gum.

Trying Something New

"**C**lass, there is an epidemic of gum chewing. It will have to stop. You all look like cows when I'm speaking to you. Come up here and throw your gum in the wastebasket."

Several children walked up to drop their gum in the basket. Robert and Paul were among them.

Mrs. Bernthal was not as strict as some teachers about gum. She just never wanted to see it. "If I see it, you lose it," she once told them.

"That's better," she said, when they set-
tled down again. "Today we are going to
talk about trying something new." Mrs. Bernthal explained how that would expand
their horizons.

"Have you ever avoided trying something new because you were afraid of it?"

Melissa Thurm raised her hand. "I didn't want to go on the roller coaster because I was afraid," she said. Melissa was afraid of everything.

"That's a very good example," said Mrs. Bernthal. "How about not trying something because you thought you wouldn't like it?"

Brian Hoberman raised his hand. "I thought I wouldn't like this book my godmother sent me. I put it on my bookshelf. I didn't want to read it. Then, one day, I was looking for something and found the book. I read the first few pages, and it sounded good. I read it and I liked it a lot."

"That's the point," said Mrs. Bernthal. "Trying something new widens your world. It gives you more choices, and you learn more about yourself."

Robert thought of his brother, Charlie, trying to teach him to shoot baskets in their driveway. It gave him the knowledge that he really wasn't good at sports.

"I want you to try something new," Mrs. Bernthal said. "Something you have never tried before. Each time you try something new, write down what you think of it. This is not homework. It's just something I want you to think about."

Robert liked things to stay the way they were. Change made him nervous. He'd give it a try for Mrs. Bernthal, but he didn't expect to like it at all.

Opposites

There are eight children at your birthday party. There are a dozen cupcakes. If you want to divide the cupcakes evenly among the children, how many cupcakes will each child get?

Robert kept getting different answers. Fractions made his head spin. He wished he had a real cupcake—with vanilla icing and colored sprinkles. One would be enough. Why did those kids need more than one cupcake, anyway? His mom would just put the rest away for another time.

From his room upstairs, Robert could hear the commotion as Charlie burst in the front door.

"We won! We won!" he shouted. Charlie was always winning, but this time, it meant his team would get to play in the statewide hockey championships.

"That's wonderful, Charlie," Robert heard his mom say.

"Way to go, Charlie," said his dad. He could imagine all the hugs and pats and backslaps going on downstairs.

Robert couldn't believe what opposites he and his brother were. Charlie was a real athlete and had trophies to prove it. Robert was always the last one picked for anybody's team. Even when he was forced to play dodgeball on the playground, he was always the first one hit and removed from the game.

The excitement over Charlie's good news was still in the air at dinnertime. Charlie gave them a blow-by-blow report on how his team creamed the other team. Robert never understood the fun in kids practically killing each other over one little hockey puck.

"And what about your day, Robert? What did you do?" His mom always tried to make him feel important, too. The trouble is, he never did anything like win a game for his team.

He told them about the bubble gum wrapper. Charlie thought that was hilarious.

"It proves you don't exist," he said. Robert knew he was teasing, but it still made him feel uncomfortable.

"I exist," he said.

"Of course you do, dear," said Mrs. Dorfman.

Charlie snickered as he dipped a french fry into a pool of ketchup.

"Also, Mrs. Bernthal wants us to try something new," he said. All three members of his family looked at him.

"Like what?" said his mom.

"Anything we haven't done before."

"Grow taller," said Charlie.

Robert's dad laughed at Charlie's humor. "That's an interesting idea," he said.

"What? Growing taller?" asked Charlie.

"No, Charlie. It's important to try new things. You learn more about yourself and what you can do, what you like, what you might want to do with your life."

"That's what Mrs. Bernthal said," added Robert. "But I don't know what to try."

"Try hockey," said Charlie, as enthusiastic about his sport as ever. "If you can get those little noodle legs of yours to hold up." He chuckled. Charlie thought he was a million laughs.

There had to be something new Robert could try that didn't involve sports. That was Charlie's specialty. Robert looked at his plate. His mom had put long, green stalks on it.

"What are these?" he asked.

"Asparagus," answered his mom.

Normally, he would just pick at them and leave them on his plate. Not this time. This was a perfect opportunity to try something new. Robert speared one of the stalks.

He brought the stalk close to his nose and smelled it. Then he licked it gently. Finally, he held his nose with his other hand and put it in his mouth, gulping it down almost without chewing. YUCCCH. It was nasty. Charlie was watching. Robert sat up straight.

"Not bad," he fibbed.

Charlie stared. "Really?"

"Really," said Robert, smiling. He picked up a chicken nugget.

Charlie went for a stalk. He put it in his mouth, and his face turned green. He looked like he might barf.

Robert giggled. He loved it when he found ways to pay his brother back for all the teasing he took from him.

The Next Picasso

Robert could now eliminate sports and strange vegetables as new things to try. What else was there? Let's see. He already knew how to take pictures since his parents had bought him a camera last year. He knew how to keep a library in good shape from being the Class Library Monitor, and how to take care of animals from the pet service he ran.

Maybe he could paint. His best friend, Paul, was a terrific artist. Paul always had such a good time making pictures. Everyone said Paul had talent. Robert didn't know if he had talent, but he would give it a try.

He took out his paint set and paper. He dipped his brush in water and shook it until it was almost dry and the bristles came to a sort of point. Miss Valentine, the art teacher, had shown them how to do that. Then he dipped it in the blue paint.

He painted a picture of children playing on the beach. He made the sky a bright, summery blue and the sand a light tan. So far, so good. He rinsed his brush, swirling it around in the water. He shook it off and dipped the brush into the white paint, so he could put a cloud in the sky. The blue paint was still wet, so the cloud became blue, too.

The children came out a little more orange than he intended. Robert thought the big red ball they were tossing to each other was a little flat on one side and tried to make it rounder. Then the other side looked wrong, so he tried to even it out.

17

First he added to one side, then to the other, until the ball was twice the size it started out to be.

As he waited for the paint to dry, Robert thought of something Miss Valentine had told them once. She had showed them pictures by several famous painters. One of the artists had put two eyes on the same side of the face. She said he did that to show a new way of looking at things. His name was Picasso, and he became very famous. Miss Valentine said any one of them could become the next Picasso.

When the painting was dry, Robert thumped downstairs to show his mother. She was reading in the living room. As she studied the picture, Charlie walked by.

"Why are those men in orange suits tossing a giant radish in the air?" he asked, continuing to sweep through the room.

Robert started to answer, but his mother jumped in.

"Your composition is very good,
Robert," she said, "and you are not afraid
to use strong colors."

Is that good? Robert wondered. His
mom was always enthusiastic about his
artwork, but Robert had a feeling it wasn't

a very good painting. He went upstairs and put away his paints and brushes.

He got ready for bed. "Good night, Flo. Good night, Billie," he said to his two turtle-doves. He slipped the cover over their cage so they would go to sleep.

"Good night, Fuzzy," Robert said to his pet tarantula in her little glass tank. He remembered when he first got Fuzzy. Susanne Lee Rodgers had asked him to take care of her when her cat started to look at Fuzzy as if she were a catnip toy. It was not easy trying to sleep that first night with Fuzzy in the room, but he soon got used to her and even grew to like her.

What else could he try that he had never done before? He thought about what other kids did. Kristi Mills took dancing lessons. Dancing? No way! He already knew he had two left feet. He didn't need to show every-body. Lester Willis built things. Robert didn't even know how to hold a hammer. Susanne Lee Rodgers had a pet cat. His parents didn't want pets that needed walking or could mess up the house. Vanessa Nicolini played the flute.

That's it! Music!

Tomorrow, he would ask Mrs. Gold, the music teacher, if he could learn to play a musical instrument. He had never done that before, and it was not as scary as sleeping in the same room with a tarantula. It might even be fun.

Tubby the Tuba

Mrs. Gold was flipping through a book when Robert walked into the music room.

"Good morning, Robert. You're early, aren't you?" She looked at her watch.

"Yes," Robert answered. "I want to ask you something."

"What is it?"

"Can I—I mean, may I play an instrument?"

Mrs. Gold took her glasses off and put them on her desk. "Well, it's a little late. Most of the instruments have been given out. What instrument did you want to play?" she asked.

Robert shrugged. "Anything," he replied.

Mrs. Gold walked to the back of the room. She uncovered a large shiny instrument that looked like a twisted horn. "This is all we have left."

"What is it?" asked Robert. He stared at the horn. It was huge.

"This is a tuba," said Mrs. Gold. "It's probably too big for you."

Suddenly, Robert remembered his mom reading to him, long ago when he was little, a story called Tubby the Tuba. She had played a CD while they read, and he heard the music that went with the story. He always loved the *OOM PUM* sound that Tubby made.

"It's not too big," he said, standing taller.

"Have you ever played an instrument before?" asked Mrs. Gold.

Robert shook his head. "No."

"Can you read music?"

"No."

"Hmmm. Well, we can try. There's an easy way to remember the names of the notes you will need," she said. She picked up a music book and opened it, pointing to the round black marks dancing across the page. "These are the notes you play. Each one is on a different line and has a name. G—B—D—F—A. You can remember 'Good Boys Deserve Fun Always.' The first letters of those words will help you remember the notes." Mrs. Gold looked at Robert. "Do you think you can remember that?"

Robert nodded. This was cool. He could remember the notes. Good Boys Deserve Fun Always. Good Boys Deserve Fun Always. He repeated the words to himself again and again.

"Now, this is how you play a G on the tuba." She showed Robert how to hold the horn and how to blow into it.

Robert tried. Nothing came out.

"You need a lot of breath to blow a note through a tuba," she said.

He tried again, harder. A sound came out, but it was more like the sound of a wounded bear than a musical instrument.

"Why don't you practice at home? I'll let you take the tuba home with you this afternoon. You can keep it there this week to see how it goes. Practice the G first. You want the note to come out smooth, not shaky."

"Thanks," said Robert.

"Come back for your instrument this afternoon. You don't want to carry it around all day."

Robert put the tuba down. "Okay," he said. He couldn't wait.

At three o'clock, Robert ran to the music room to collect his tuba. Mrs. Gold was waiting for him. "Have fun, Robert." She had put the tuba in a battered black case that was almost bigger than Robert.

"I will. Thanks," he shouted back as he tried to run for the school bus. It was difficult, with the big black case in his arms and his book bag on his back. He usually walked home with Paul, but with the tuba to carry, he had to ride.

"I'll go with you," said Paul, when he heard about the tuba.

Lester was there when Robert and Paul got to the bus.

"Yo, Rob," said Lester. "What's THAT?"

"Hi," said Robert. "It's a tuba."

"You'll probably have to pay extra for taking up two seats."

Robert tried to smile. Even though he and Lester were sort of friends, now, Robert didn't want to say anything that could make Lester mad. Lester was too big and strong.

Jesse Meiner whistled as Robert bumped his way down the aisle to find a seat.

"What have you got there?" he yelled. "A dead body?" The other kids snickered.

"Yeah, a real fat one, all curled up," shouted Lester.

Robert went all the way to the back and set the tuba case down in the aisle. Paul sat down on the seat next to him. He opened his book bag and took out two pieces of Bubble-oney bubble gum. He handed one to Robert.

"How come you picked the tuba?" he asked.

"It was all that was left," Robert answered, peeling the wrapper off his gum.

"Awesome," said Paul.

"Yeah," said Robert. "What did you get?" He leaned over to see.

"No number," said Paul. "And my fortune says: *'Tomorrow will bring good news.'*" He crumpled his wrapper. "What's yours?"

There was no number on Robert's wrapper, either. His fortune read: *"You can do anything you set your mind to."*

Robert leaned back, seeing himself in a red uniform with gold buttons down the front, playing the biggest horn in a marching band.

"Cool," he said.

New things I tried

new thing	what I think
1. asparrigus	IT STINKS!
2. painting	I STINK!
3. playing the tuba	Cool!

Practice

OOOOOMMMMMFFFFF.

"What was that?" Charlie came running to Robert's room and looked in.

Robert looked up from the huge instrument. "It's a G," he said.

"A what? " Charlie came closer. "What is that?" he cried. "And why does it sound so bad?"

"It's a tuba. And I have to practice," Robert answered, going back to his G note. OOOOOOOOMP.

Charlie covered his ears and left.

Every day, after he did his homework, Robert worked on the G note. It took a lot of wind. When he had no breath left, or his lip needed a rest, he stopped for a while. Then he started again. He played the G note over and over again until he got it nearly right. He was sure Mrs. Gold would be pleased with his progress.

On Saturday, Paul came over with his bike. "Are you ready?" he asked.

"Sure," said Robert. He was happy to take a break from blowing G notes on the tuba.

They rode over to Van Saun Park. They knew a way through the streets to avoid the main roads. They stopped at the pond and rested their bikes as they watched people feed the ducks. Paul took two pieces of bubble gum out of his pocket. He handed one to Robert. They opened them at the same time.

Neither of them had a number printed on his wrapper. Again.

"We're going broke buying this gum," said Paul.

"Yeah," said Robert. "Do you think there are ANY numbers printed on these wrappers?"

"I don't know," said Paul. "What's your fortune?"

Robert pretended to read, "Help. I'm a prisoner in a bubble gum factory."

Paul cracked up. "What does it really say?" he asked.

"It says, *'You are a person of many facets.'*"

"What's a facet?" asked Paul.

Robert shrugged. "It's what water comes out of."

"No," said Paul, "that's a faucet." He shrugged and continued reading. " *'Mighty oaks from little acorns grow.'*" Paul looked up. "Who are they calling a little acorn?" said Paul.

"Yeah. Everybody knows you're a big nut."

Laughing, they got on their bikes and rode through the park, blowing bubbles.

That night after dinner, Robert picked up the tuba and tried the G note again.

OOOOOM.

OOO-OOOOOOOOM.

OOM-OOM-OOMMMM

OOOOOOEEEEEOOOOOM.

After about three minutes, Charlie burst into his room. "How can a person study with that noise?"

"Sorry," said Robert, "but I have to practice." He couldn't understand why the sound of the tuba was bothering Charlie. His brother always had music playing in his headphones, even when he did his homework.

"Maybe you need to practice somewhere nobody can hear you—like out in the middle of the ocean!" Charlie threw up his hands and left. Robert heard him thump downstairs.

He blew into the mouthpiece again, harder this time. *OOOOOMMM*. He had to admit, it did sound a little like a cow mooing.

The Band

On Monday, Robert lugged the tuba to the music room.

"Hey, Robert, why did you bring the dead body back to school?" cried Lester, who passed him in the hall. "How come you didn't bury it?"

Robert just smiled and ignored Lester's remark. Mrs. Gold was happy to hear he had been practicing. He took the tuba out of its case and waited for Mrs. Gold to hear him play.

"Robert, I'd like to hear you but I've got a class coming in a couple of minutes. Can you come back this afternoon to show me? I'm sure Mrs. Bernthal won't mind."

"Sure," said Robert. He put the tuba in the back of the room where he had first seen it.

Robert felt important. The other kids would surely notice when he got a pass to go to the music room. Robert couldn't wait.

In the afternoon, when they had finished their math work, Mrs. Bernthal let Robert go to the music room.

Robert took the tuba and played the G note for Mrs. Gold. It took all his breath, but Mrs. Gold was pleased. "You must have practiced a lot," she said. "Continue to practice, Robert. Take the tuba home with you again. Learn the B note. Once you can play both the G and the B, you can come to band practice."

"Really?" It was hard to believe. He was going to play with the school band!

"Really."

"Thanks," he said.

When Robert came home with the tuba, his mother met him at the door.

"Robert. You brought the tuba home." She seemed a little surprised. "I thought you were going to leave it at school from now on."

"Mrs. Gold said I did a good job learning the G," said Robert. "Now I have to learn the B. She said I can keep it at home for another week."

Robert thought he heard a strange sound coming from his mother, but when he turned to face her, she looked okay. He struggled upstairs with his tuba and began to practice the B.

Ear Plugs

OOOOOM.
OO-UR-OOO.
OOO-ROO-ROOMP.
OOOOOOOOOOMMMMMMMMMM.

Ah. At last. Robert felt the note—the B—right down to his toes. It was strong, the way Mrs. Gold liked it to sound.

He was just about to play the notes again when he heard his brother's heavy footsteps thumping up the stairs. He put the tuba on his bed. No sense in having another scene with Charlie. He had practiced enough for the day. Besides, he was hungry. Dinner should be ready soon. He went downstairs to check it out.

"Hi, Dad," he said as he passed his dad, sitting in his recliner reading the newspaper. His dad didn't answer.

"Dad?" he said a little louder. There was still no answer.

Robert went right up to him and tapped the newspaper. His father jumped.

"What? Oh, Robert! Hi, Tiger. What's up?" He took something out of his ears.

"I just said hi," said Robert.

"Oh." He smiled. "I . . . I didn't hear you," he said.

Robert went to the kitchen. His mom was slicing a tomato. He loved tomatoes. He asked if he could have the end. His mom didn't answer.

"Mom? MOM?"

She turned to him and stopped slicing.

"Yes, Robert?" She wiped her hands on a towel and took ear plugs out of her ears.

Oh, that's what's going on.

"I just wanted a slice of tomato," he said. Was he driving them all crazy with his playing? His mom slid the end of the tomato across the cutting board toward him. Robert picked it up and popped it in his mouth.

Well, if he was going to play the tuba, he had to practice, didn't he? Someday they would realize it was worth it. They would see him march, wearing his red uniform with the gold buttons, playing his tuba. They would be so proud!

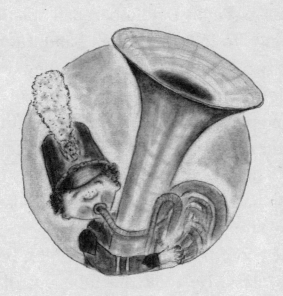

Sour Note

It was Assembly Day. Robert had practiced enough to join the school band. He had only two notes to play, but they were good, strong notes. Near the end of the second page of music, he had to play the G and the B. He could do it if he paid attention to his cue. He had practiced every day. His lip had probably grown a new muscle.

He stopped to leave his tuba in the music room before he went to Mrs. Bernthal's class. He took the tuba out of its case and polished the shiny brass with his sleeve. Then he propped it in a corner of the room. He wanted it to be ready for him when he came back later to get it. Assembly was at nine o'clock.

Mrs. Bernthal marked the attendance and asked everyone to take out their spelling notebooks. "Matt, I saw your gum. Come up here and throw it in the wastebasket, please."

Matt Blakey got up slowly and dragged himself to the front of the room. He wrapped his gum in a scrap of paper and threw it away. Robert made extra sure he didn't chew his gum so it showed.

"Here are your new spelling words for today," said Mrs. Bernthal. "Everyone write them down, please." She wrote the words on the chalkboard, and the children copied them.

cocoon	magnet
victory	reptile
wealthy	culture
journal	prowl
absent	feather

Robert had only copied eight of them when he looked at his watch. It was five minutes to nine. Quickly, he wrote down the last two words and closed his notebook.

Mrs. Bernthal had given him and Vanessa permission to leave early to join the others in the band. "Good luck!" she whispered to them.

Vanessa had cut her hair really short. Robert almost didn't recognize her at first.

"Your hair. It's different," he said.

Vanessa's hand went up to her hair as though she wanted to be sure the rest was still there. "I got bubble gum in it for the second time, and my mom got so mad she cut it short."

"Wow!" was all Robert could think of to say. Then he added, "It looks nice."

Vanessa smiled. "Thanks," she said.

There were some older kids in the music room when they got there. Robert didn't recognize them as members of the band. They must be there to practice. Some of them snickered as he picked up the tuba. He checked to see that his pants were zipped and there was nothing trailing from his shoe, but they continued to laugh.

What was so funny? Maybe they thought he looked funny, this little kid carrying the big horn. He carried the tuba out the door, and he and Vanessa walked down the hall to the auditorium.

"Don't let them bother you," said Vanessa.

Robert looked at her. "I won't," he answered. He was glad he wasn't the only one who felt the snickering was directed at him.

"Man, look at that," he heard a fifth grader say as they passed each other in the hall. Another fifth grader smiled. You never knew about older kids. Sometimes they could be nice.

Robert had never had fifth graders even notice him before. They made him uncomfortable just a few minutes ago, but now they made him feel special, and handsome, like he was already wearing that red-and-gold uniform.

The band members were assembled in front of the auditorium, right below the stage. Mrs. Gold gave them last-minute instructions. Robert took his place on a chair behind the others. Vanessa was near the front with her flute.

He set up his music on the stand in front of him. Even with only two notes to play, he had to follow the music the others played. Mrs. Gold explained to him that a band worked together as a team. Ha! Charlie would get a laugh out of that! Robert being on a team of any kind!

He picked up the tuba and put his mouth on the mouthpiece. Uh-oh. He still had his bubble gum in his mouth. He couldn't get up and throw it away now, so he'd have to swallow it. He gulped and swallowed three times before the gum was gone.

The first graders arrived first and filled up the front rows. Behind them sat the second graders, many of them with front teeth missing. The third and fourth grade classes came next, seating themselves right behind the second graders. Finally, the oldest kids in the school, the fifth graders, came in, taking up the back rows. Robert noticed the same bunch of boys who had been in the music room sitting together, still laughing among themselves. They sure thought something was funny.

Mrs. Gold gave the signal by holding up her baton. The children stood up. On the downbeat, the band played and the children sang the first notes of "The Star-Spangled Banner." Robert watched for his cue. He had to come in right after ". . . that our flag was still there. . . ." He got ready as the music came closer to his cue.

The voices rang out, ". . . gave proof through the night . . ." Robert took a deep breath. ". . . that our flag was still there."

In the midst of the sounds of violins, a flute, a drum, and a clarinet, came the most awful sound—like a gigantic truck chugging uphill and squealing at the same time. The singing stopped. The band stopped. Robert, his cheeks sore from blowing his horn, sat startled, like everyone else. Then laughter rippled through the auditorium, with a few whistles coming from the back. Mrs. Gold glared at Robert as she signaled frantically for the children to finish the song.

After Assembly, the children took their instruments and went back to the music room. Mrs. Gold followed them in.

"What in the world happened, Robert?"

Robert gulped. "I don't know," he replied.

"Let's take a look at that instrument," she said. She took the tuba from Robert's arms and looked inside. Suddenly, Robert wondered if he had really swallowed his bubble gum or if he had dropped it into the tuba.

"I can't see anything," said Mrs. Gold.

Robert thought his heart would stop beating. What if his big wad of sticky bubble gum was down there? What if he had ruined the instrument? All his hard work would have been for nothing. And Mrs. Gold would never let him play the tuba again.

She reached into the horn and pulled out a crumpled paper lunch bag. Horrified, Robert watched as she reached in again and pulled out a crushed juice carton. She looked in.

"I can't see anything else," she said. "It's too curvy. But I will have to get this cleaned out." For a moment, Robert had a picture of those fifth graders in the music room that morning. So that's what was so funny! But he didn't want to be a tattletale, so he didn't say anything.

"I'm sorry, Robert." She put the tuba down. "Who knows what else is down there?" she continued. "We'll have to find something else for you to play, maybe in the new string ensemble."

Robert realized with a jolt that his tuba-playing career was over. So were his dreams of marching in a band in a red-and-gold uniform.

Walking home from school, Paul unwrapped two new pieces of bubble gum. Robert read his wrapper. No number. Again. Robert was used to that. He never won anything, except once, when he won a certificate from Mrs. Bernthal for taking care of the class library. *"Expect the unexpected,"* his fortune said. Hadn't he had enough of the unexpected already? "What's yours?" he asked Paul.

"No number. And my fortune is: *'You are a person of character.'*"

"That's true," said Robert. "You sure are a character!" He laughed at his own joke, and Paul laughed with him.

Lumpfish and
Frogs' Eyes

"**N**o more tuba?" Robert's mom said with surprise. "How come?"

Robert told her the story.

"Robert, that's terrible! Who would stuff garbage in a horn?"

Charlie yelled from the living room, "I would, if it were Robert's!"

"Charlie, go do your homework." Charlie got up and went upstairs, snickering.

"Maybe when the tuba is fixed you can play it again." Robert imagined someone with a huge vacuum cleaner trying to

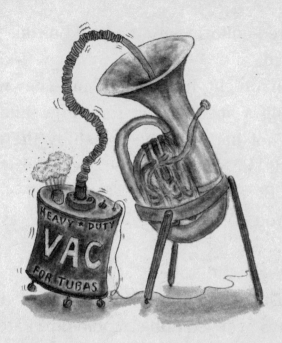

clean out the tuba. But Mrs. Gold had said she would find him a different instrument.

When Robert's dad came home, he, too, tried to comfort Robert. "Don't worry, Tiger. You'll find something else that you'll love just as much."

Robert wasn't sure about that. He had really grown to love the tuba. His dream of playing in a marching band and wearing the red uniform with the gold buttons was ruined.

That night, he phoned Paul. They were having a spelling test tomorrow, and he had not had a chance to study the new words. He was playing in the band when Mrs. Bernthal went over them in class.

"You copied them down, right?" asked Paul.

"Yes," said Robert.

"Then study them. You'll be okay." Paul always believed Robert could do whatever he set out to do.

"Okay," he said. He went over those words until he could spell them in his sleep. It kept him from thinking about the tuba.

The next day, Robert sailed through his spelling test. For a moment, he wasn't sure if COCOON had one C in the middle or two, but he wrote it down both ways and liked the one with one C better.

It was a shock when he got his paper back. He stared at two words, PROUL and FETHER.

"Pssst, Paul," whispered Robert, across the table. "Can I see your paper?"

Paul slid his paper across to Robert. He had 100 in red at the top of the page. All of his words were correct. Robert looked for PROUL and FETHER. His stomach tightened. He saw PROWL and FEATHER instead, checked off as correct.

He opened his notebook to where he had written the spelling words. "Oh, no!" he cried. Those were the last two words he had copied. He was in a hurry to get to Assembly, and he had copied them wrong.

Robert was sitting with his head in his hands when a voice came over the PA system. It was Mr. Lipkin, the principal. "Boys and girls, the problem of bubble gum in this school has become a major disaster. From now on, if you are caught chewing bubble gum in the school building you will be sent to my office and your parents will have to come to school."

Robert sat up straight.

"If bubble gum is found on you, or even in your desk or book bag, you will be punished. We must stop this nonsense now!" The PA system clicked off.

Robert nearly fell off his chair. "Paul! We have a gazillion pieces of bubble gum in our book bags!"

"We'll get rid of it at recess," Paul said. "Bring your book bag."

The clock moved slowly, but recess finally came. Robert and Paul grabbed their book bags. Susanne Lee Rodgers saw them.

"What are you taking your book bags for? We're only going to recess."

"Um . . ." said Robert. "I have a snack in mine."

"Me, too," said Paul.

"What kind of snack?" asked Susanne Lee.

"Oh, nothing you would like," said Robert quickly. He made sure the zipper on his bag was closed.

"How do you know I wouldn't like it?" asked Susanne Lee. "What is it?"

"Lumpfish!" said Paul, just as quickly.

Robert couldn't help laughing, so he turned away.

"That's disgusting," said Susanne Lee. "What about you?" she asked Robert. "You have lumpfish, too?" She had her hands on her hips now.

"I have frogs' eyes," said Robert. "They're very nutritious." Now it was Paul who had to turn away before they gave the whole thing away.

"We have to have some every day . . ." yelled Paul, as he ran from the classroom.

". . . or we'll die!" shouted Robert, running after him.

They never looked back to see the expression on Susanne Lee's face, but Robert could imagine it. She always looked at them as though they were worms.

"Lumpfish!" said Robert, when they finally got outside. "How did you think of that?"

"I saw it on a jar once, in a fancy store."

They ran to the far end of the school yard, opened their book bags, and took out all their gum. Quickly, they ripped off the wrappers to see if they had won any money. They hadn't. They threw it all into a trash barrel.

It hurt to see all that bubble gum go to waste. It must have cost them four dollars. It would be worth it if they ever won anything, but it was beginning to look like that would never happen.

Like Asparagus

The next day, Mrs. Gold asked Robert to join her new group of violin students. There were seven of them learning to play the instrument. Someone had dropped out, so there was an instrument available.

Robert looked at the violin. It was okay, but he couldn't imagine himself playing it in a marching band in a parade. He learned how to hold it and how to use the bow. He had to play the notes by holding down different strings as he pulled the bow across them.

Their first practice session made quite a racket, but nobody seemed to mind. At home, everyone would probably hate him for bringing home another noisy instrument to play. He decided to leave the violin in school and practice there, whenever he could.

In spite of his efforts, Robert just couldn't learn to love the violin. He missed the tuba, which had felt like a friend to him. The violin scratched and squeaked, making him wince with every note.

One evening Robert's mom and dad suggested they go out for pizza instead of ordering in, as they usually did.

"Can we go to Pete's?" asked Robert.

"Sure," said his mom. "We haven't been there in a while. I'm sure we'd all like to see Pepperoni."

Robert smiled. He always liked to see Pepperoni.

Pepperoni was a big yellow Labrador retriever, a dog Robert had helped to train for the Happy Valley Animal Shelter. Robert loved that dog, even though he knew he had to give him up one day, when the dog had been housebroken and learned some manners. And Pete was a great owner, because he loved dogs and ran a pizza restaurant, and Pepperoni was crazy about pizza.

When they got to the restaurant, Pete gave them a big welcome. He called for Pepperoni to come out from the back and say hello, but the dog didn't come.

"What's the matter with that dog?" he said. "Let's go see." He opened the gate and let them all go past the kitchen into a small back room. Over in a corner was a cardboard box with two adorable puppies inside on a baby blanket. Pepperoni stood over them, as though he were protecting them. Robert could have sworn Pepperoni was smiling.

"Good boy," he said, kneeling down and giving Pepperoni a big hug. "What's this? Whose puppies are these?"

Pete smiled. "You have to ask? That is the proud papa right there," he said. Pepperoni's tail *thump, thumped* on the floor.

Robert couldn't believe it. "Where is their mother?" he asked.

"She lives in the house next door to us," said Pete. "She's a beautiful German shepherd. She had six puppies. Her family let me take these two to work so I could show them off. All six puppies are going to need homes."

Robert's heart ached when he heard that. He picked up one pup, who was climbing on the back of the other one. He looked exactly like Pepperoni, only smaller.

Robert's parents had made it very clear about no dogs. He had been trying to break them down for years, without success. The closest he ever got was being allowed to train Pepperoni for the shelter.

Finally, Robert's family went to the dining room and sat in their favorite booth. Pepperoni had to stay in the back. While they waited for their order, Robert's dad asked about his latest "something new"—the violin.

"It's okay," he said. "Not like the tuba, though."

"Trying something new doesn't mean you have to like it. Sometimes it's a good way of finding out you don't like something, or it's not for you."

"Like asparagus?" asked Robert.

"Yes, like asparagus. The idea is to try as many new things as possible and make choices."

"I wanted to like the violin," Robert said. "Other kids seem to get the bow and the fingering, but I just get tangled up. I even hate the sound when I'm practicing."

Charlie started to say something, but Mrs. Dorfman glared at him and he stopped.

"The thing about music, or art, or anything creative," said Robert's mom, "is that you have to really love it to do it well. If your heart isn't in it, there's no point in persisting. Would you like to give up the violin?"

Robert didn't want to seem too eager, or they would think he hadn't given it much thought. But he had. He thought about it all the time. "Yes," he said. "I would."

"Well, okay, then," said his mom. "Explain to Mrs. Gold just as you explained to us. I'm sure she will understand."

Robert felt the relief wash over him. "Maybe I'll change my mind about the violin someday," he said. "But I really wish I could play the tuba again. I really like it a lot." Charlie groaned.

"Right," said his mom. His dad nodded in agreement, giving Charlie a look.

After they stuffed themselves with pizza, Robert wanted to stop one more time to say good-bye to Pepperoni.

"Let's all go," said Mr. Dorfman. They walked single file to the back room.

Robert picked up the puppy that looked like Pepperoni and rubbed his cheek against his soft, silky fur. His parents watched from the doorway, whispering to each other.

"Robert . . ." said his mom. "Would you like to have that puppy for your own?"

Robert wasn't sure he heard right. He looked at his father.

"Yes, Tiger," said his father. "We've been thinking. It's time you had that dog you've always wanted. You've certainly proved yourself responsible."

Robert couldn't say anything. It was too good to be true. Not letting go of the puppy, he stood up. His brain seemed to have gone dead. But he must have heard right. He was taking the puppy home!

Pete could not have been happier. "Well, you're taking Junior home, yes?" Robert nodded, hugging the puppy. "I know this is right," said Pete, "because you did such a wonderful job with Pepperoni."

Robert's voice came back, and he said, "Thanks!" While his parents said good-bye to Pete, he hurried ahead with his puppy. He wanted to be sure they didn't change their minds.

At Last

T he next morning, Saturday, Paul came over to meet the new puppy. They played with it and watched it explore Robert's room.

They opened two new pieces of bubble gum as they watched the puppy play on the floor with a squeak toy. Robert's wrapper had the number "1" on it. "Congratulations," it said. "You are a winner. Take this wrapper to the store where you purchased your bubble gum. The proprietor will give you the number of dollars printed here."

"One dollar!" cried Robert.

"A stinking dollar!" added Paul.

"We spent a lot more than a dollar on all the gum we bought."

The gum didn't taste so good after that. They both wrapped their wads in the wrappers and tossed them in the wastebasket.

A few more minutes passed, while they watched the puppy scramble after his toy.

"Well, I guess I should go get my dollar," said Robert. "But this time I won't buy more gum. I'll get a treat for my puppy instead. Want to come?" he asked Paul.

"Sure."

"Great. You can help me think about names for the puppy on the way."

They walked off toward the store. Running along ahead at the end of a brand-new leash, on his tiny puppy legs, was, at last, Robert's very own dog.

New things I tried

New thing	what I think
1. asparrigus	IT STINKS!
2. painting	I STINK!
3. playing the tuba	Cool!
4. playing the violin	Not Cool
5. a puppy	THE BEST!!!

BARBARA SEULING is a well-known author of fiction and nonfiction books for children, including several books about Robert. She divides her time between New York City and Vermont.

PAUL BREWER likes to draw gross, silly situations, which is why he enjoys working on books about Robert so much. He lives in San Diego, California, with his wife and two daughters.